WITHDRAWN

Jefferson Twp. Public Library
1031 Weldon Road
Oak Ridge, N.J. 07438
973-208-6244
www.jeffersonlibrary.net

APR

OKLAHOMA CITY Thunder

Jefferson Twp. Public Library
1031 Weldon Road
Oak Ridge, NJ 07438
973-208-6244
www.jeffersonlibrary.net

BY MAXWELL HAMMER

Published by The Child's World®
1980 Lookout Drive • Mankato, MN 56003-1705
800-599-READ • www.childsworld.com

Acknowledgments
The Child's World®: Mary Berendes, Publishing Director
Red Line Editorial: Editorial direction
The Design Lab: Design
Amnet: Production

Design elements: PhotoDisc, Viorika Prikhodko/iStockphoto

Photographs ©: Tony Gutierrez/AP Images, cover, title; Mark J. Terrill/AP Images, 5; The Canadian Press, Frank Gunn/AP Images, 6; Fred Jewell/AP Images, 9; Sue Ogrocki/AP Images, 10, 13, 25, 26; Bill Chan/AP Images, 17; Ted S. Warren/AP Images, 18; Jeff Roberson/AP Images, 21; Christobal Perez/AP Images, 22

Copyright © 2014 by The Child's World®
All rights reserved. No part of this book may be reproduced or utilized in any form or by any means without written permission from the publisher.

ISBN 978-1623234980
LCCN 2013931370

Printed in the United States of America
Mankato, MN
July, 2013
PA02171

About the Author

Maxwell Hammer is an author from the Adirondacks in upstate New York. He used to write about college basketball for a newspaper before turning his focus to Olympic sports and writing books. Hammer's favorite NBA team and favorite animal share the same name: Timberwolves.

Table of Contents

4 Go, Thunder!
7 Who Are the Thunder?
8 Where They Came From
11 Who They Play
12 Where They Play
15 The Basketball Court
16 Big Days
19 Tough Days
20 Meet the Fans
23 Heroes Then . . .
24 Heroes Now . . .
27 Gearing Up
28 *Sports Stats*
30 *Glossary*
31 *Find Out More*
32 *Index*

Go, Thunder!

Oklahoma has long been a state known for its college sports teams. Not anymore! The Thunder became Oklahoma's lone major pro sports team in 2008. The second smallest city in the league quickly made itself known. The Thunder became one of the hottest teams in the league. Both the players and the fans get high marks. Come on down to Oklahoma and learn about this exciting young team!

Kevin Durant (35) is a superstar scorer.

Who Are the Thunder?

The Oklahoma City Thunder play in the National Basketball Association (NBA). They are one of 30 teams in the NBA. The NBA includes the Eastern Conference and the Western Conference. The Thunder play in the Northwest Division of the Western Conference. The winner of the Eastern Conference plays the winner of the Western Conference in the **NBA Finals**. The Thunder reached the NBA Finals in 2012.

Russell Westbrook runs the Thunder's offense.

Where They Came From

The Thunder organization has a long, rich history. Most of it took place outside of Oklahoma. The team began in 1967 as the Seattle SuperSonics. The team known as the Sonics won the 1979 NBA title. It reached the NBA Finals two other times. In 2008, the team moved to Oklahoma City. It found a good home there. Local fans had shown their passion for the NBA a few years earlier. The New Orleans Hornets played the 2005–06 and 2006–07 seasons in Oklahoma City. Their hometown needed to recover after Hurricane Katrina.

Dennis Johnson helped the Seattle SuperSonics win the 1979 championship.

Who They Play

The Thunder play 82 games each season. That's a lot of basketball! They play every other NBA team at least once each season. They play teams in their division and conference more often. The old Seattle SuperSonics had a big **rivalry** with the Portland Trail Blazers. They were the only teams in the Pacific Northwest. After moving, the team developed new rivalries. Thunder fans get up for games against nearby teams such as the Dallas Mavericks and the Memphis Grizzlies.

Kevin Durant drives to the hoop against the Memphis Grizzlies.

Where They Play

The Thunder play home games at the Chesapeake Energy Arena. It is one of the liveliest arenas in the NBA! More than 18,000 fans fit in the arena for Thunder games. And it is usually sold out. Sometimes the team passes out T-shirts to fans for big games. The crowd turns into a sea of blue! No matter what, though, the fans are always loud. More than 1 million fans visit Chesapeake Energy Arena each year for Thunder games, music concerts, or other events.

Thunder fans at Chesapeake Energy Arena wore matching shirts at the 2012 NBA Finals.

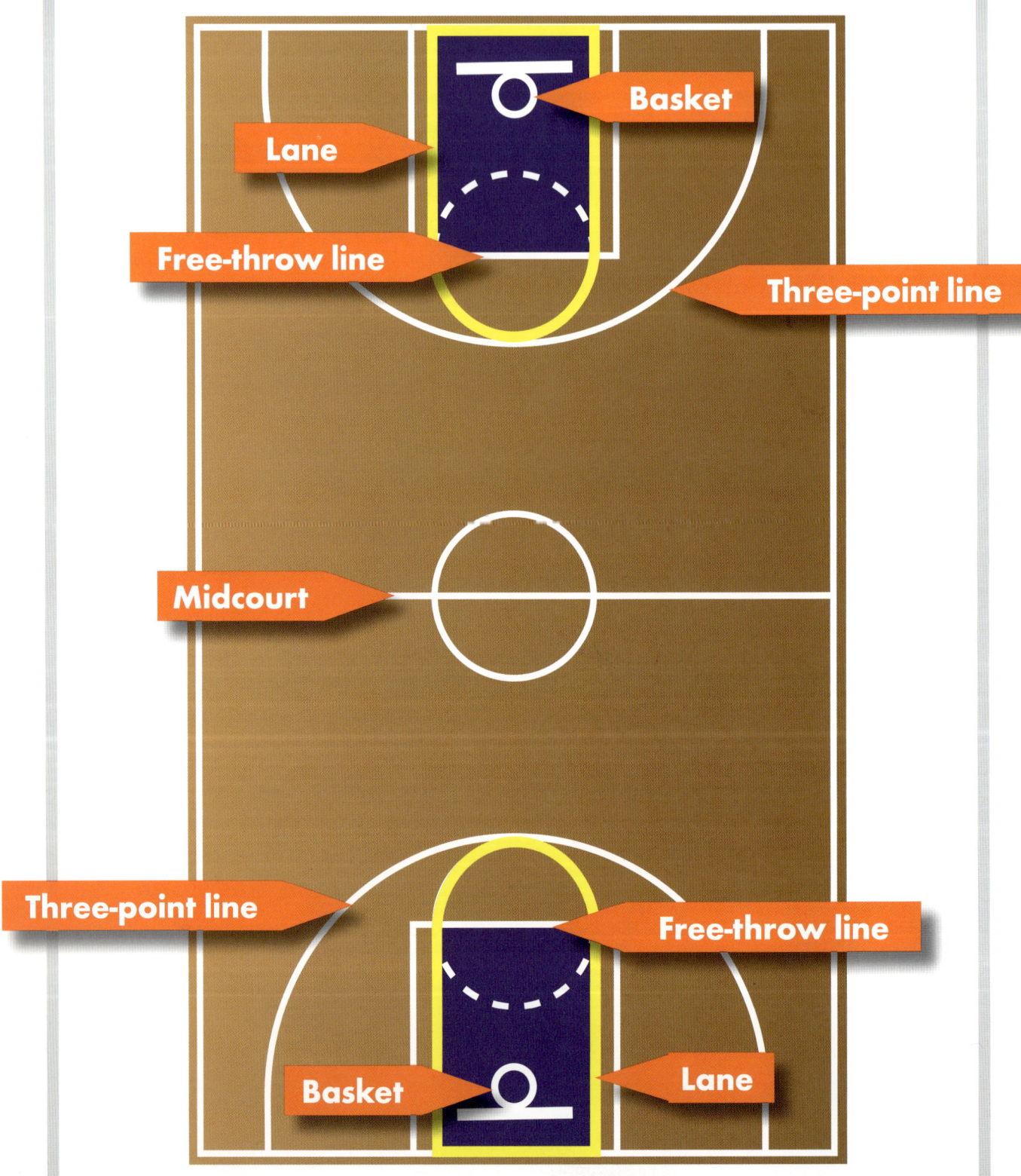

The Basketball Court

Basketball is played on a court made of wood. An NBA court is 94 feet (29 m) long. A painted line shows the middle of the court. Other lines lay out the free-throw area. The space below each basket is known as the "lane." The baskets at each end are 10 feet (3 m) off the ground. The metal rims of the baskets stick out over the court. Nylon nets hang from the rims.

Big Days

The Oklahoma City Thunder have had many great moments in their history. Here are three of the greatest:

1979: The Seattle SuperSonics cruised to the NBA championship. They beat the Washington Bullets 4–1 in the NBA Finals.

1996: Stars Gary Payton and Shawn Kemp led the Sonics to a team-record 64 wins and a trip to the NBA Finals.

2012: In just their fourth year in Oklahoma City, the Thunder reached the NBA Finals!

Gary Payton (top) battles for a rebound with Michael Jordan during the 1996 NBA Finals.

Tough Days

The Thunder can't win all their games. Some games or seasons don't turn out well. The players keep trying to play their best, though. Here are some of the toughest seasons in the team's history:

1974: The SuperSonics missed the **playoffs** for the seventh time in their first seven years. They made it the next year, though.

1999: Ouch! The Sonics won just half of their games. One year earlier they won almost 75 percent.

2008: The Sonics won just 20 games—the fewest in team history. It was also the team's last season in Seattle.

Kevin Durant gets blocked in 2008, the Sonics' last year in Seattle.

Meet the Fans

NBA fans are usually a bit more relaxed than college sports fans. They tend to sit back and watch the games rather than actively cheering. That is not the case in Oklahoma City. Thunder fans are some of the most passionate in the NBA. They often stand and loudly cheer throughout games. These fans make Oklahoma City an exciting place to see an NBA game. They also make it a tough place for opposing teams to win!

Thunder fans dance outside the arena before Game 1 of the 2012 NBA Finals.

Heroes Then...

The best basketball players ever are in the Basketball Hall of Fame. Four former SuperSonics were in the hall prior to 2013. **Point guard** Lenny Wilkens was the first. He was a great playmaker for the SuperSonics from 1968–69 to 1971–72. He later led the Sonics to the 1979 NBA title as a coach. Seattle came close to winning another NBA title in 1996. Point guard Gary Payton and **forward** Shawn Kemp led the way. Payton was a great **defender**. He guarded players so closely he became known as "The Glove." Kemp was very athletic. He was one of the best **rebounders** and shot-blockers in team history.

Shawn Kemp used his athleticism to get above opponents.

Heroes Now . . .

Few can score like forward Kevin Durant. In fact, he led the NBA in scoring average three years in a row, beginning in 2009–10. Many consider him to be the best offensive player in the NBA. Point guard Russell Westbrook is also a top scorer. He and Durant have been one of the NBA's top offensive duos since 2008–09. Forward Serge Ibaka is another Thunder star. He is a tough defender. No player had more **blocks** than Ibaka in 2011 and 2012.

Serge Ibaka drives to the rim.

Gearing Up

Oklahoma City Thunder players wear the team's uniform and special basketball sneakers. Some wear other pads to protect themselves. Check out this picture of Kendrick Perkins and learn about what NBA players wear.

THE BASKETBALL

NBA basketballs are made of leather. Several pieces are held together with rubber edges. Inside the leather ball is a hollow ball of rubber. This is filled with air. The leather is covered with little bumps called "pebbles." The pebbles help players get a good grip on the ball. The basketball used in the Women's National Basketball Association (WNBA) is slightly smaller than the men's basketball.

Kendrick Perkins is a stud under the basket.

SPORTS STATS

Note: All numbers shown are through the 2012–13 season.

HIGH SCORERS
These players have scored the most points for the Thunder.

PLAYER	POINTS
Gary Payton	18,207
Fred Brown	14,018

HELPING HAND
Here are the Thunder's all-time leaders in **assists**.

PLAYER	ASSISTS
Gary Payton	7,384
Nate McMillan	4,893

MOST THREE-POINT SHOTS MADE

Shots taken from behind a line about 23 feet (7 m) from the basket are worth three points. Here are the Thunder's best at these long-distance shots.

PLAYER	THREE-POINT BASKETS
Rashard Lewis	973
Gary Payton	917

CLEANING THE BOARDS

Rebounds are a big part of the game. Here are the Thunder's best rebounders.

PLAYER	REBOUNDS
Jack Sikma	7,729
Shawn Kemp	5,978

COACH

Who coached the Thunder to the most wins?

Lenny Wilkens, 478

GLOSSARY

assists passes to teammates that lead directly to making a basket

blocks when a defender stops a shot before it reaches the basket

defender a player who is trying to stop the other team from scoring when it has the ball

forward one of two tall players who rebound and score near the basket

NBA Finals the seven-game NBA championship series, in which the champion must win four games

playoffs a series of games between 16 teams that decides which two teams will play in the NBA Finals

point guard the team's main ball handler, who brings the ball up the court and sets up the offense

rebounders players who grab rebounds, which are missed shots that bounce off the backboard or rim

rebounds missed shots that bounce off the backboard or rim and are grabbed by another player

rivalry an ongoing competition between teams that play each other often, over a long time

FIND OUT MORE

BOOKS

Frisch, Aaron. *Oklahoma City Thunder*. Mankato, MN: Creative Education, 2012.

Hareas, John. *Championship Teams*. New York: Scholastic, 2010.

Smallwood, John N. *Megastars*. New York: Scholastic, 2011.

WEB SITES

Visit our Web page for links about the Oklahoma City Thunder and other NBA teams: **childsworld.com/links**

Note to Parents, Teachers, and Librarians: We routinely verify our Web links to make sure they are safe and active sites. So encourage your readers to check them out!

INDEX

assists, 28
basketball court diagram, 14
Basketball Hall of Fame, 23
baskets, 15
Brooks, Scott, 29
Brown, Fred, 28
Chesapeake Energy Arena, 12
coaches, 23, 29
college sports, 4, 20
Dallas Mavericks, 11
defense, 23, 24
Durant, Kevin, 24
Eastern Conference, 7
fans, 4, 8, 11, 12, 20
forward, 23, 24
free-throw area, 15
history, 4, 7, 8, 16, 19, 23, 24
Hurricane Katrina, 8
Ibaka, Serge, 24
Kemp, Shawn, 16, 23, 29
lane, 15
Lewis, Rashard, 29
McMillan, Nate, 28
Memphis Grizzlies, 11
NBA championship, 8, 16, 23
NBA Finals, 7, 8, 16
New Orleans Hornets, 8
Northwest Division, 7
Payton, Gary, 16, 23, 28, 29
Perkins, Kendrick, 27
playoffs, 19
point guard, 23, 24
Portland Trail Blazers, 11
rebounds, 23, 29
rivals, 11
Seattle SuperSonics, 8, 11, 16, 19, 23
Sikma, Jack, 29
three-point shots, 29
uniforms, 27
Washington Bullets, 16
Westbrook, Russell, 24
Western Conference, 7
Wilkens, Lenny, 23, 29
Women's National Basketball Association (WNBA), 27
worst season, 19